# The State of Us
# Charlie Hill

First published April 2023 by Fly on the Wall Press

Published in the UK by

Fly on the Wall Press

56 High Lea Rd

New Mills

Derbyshire

SK22 3DP

www.flyonthewallpress.co.uk

ISBN: 9781915789020

Copyright Charlie Hill © 2023

A CIP Catalogue record for this book is available from the British Library.

Printed in the UK by Severn, Gloucester on responsibly sourced paper

MIX
Paper from
responsible sources
FSC® C022174

*This one's for you, son...*

# CONTENTS

# CONTENTS

# WORK

For weeks after the detonations, the two men worked together, Burt moving things and Bill counting things. They worked inside and outside, although it was sometimes difficult to tell the difference. Bill carried a torch which they used inside when the power was off, or outside when the sun was hidden.

One day, or perhaps it was night, the two men sat in a building on a pile of things. They were wearing body suits but had taken their face masks off and were eating and talking. Bill was cheery, Burt distracted.

"What have you got?" said Bill.

"Dried meat," said Burt.

"Me too," said Bill. "It's good isn't it?"

"I wouldn't go that far. It's dried meat, isn't it?"

"At least we have dried meat," said Bill, 'that's something to be thankful for. Some people don't, you know."

"I suppose so," said Burt. "But when I eat dried meat I'm reminded of moving things."

"What do you mean?"

"I'm reminded of moving things. I do it because it sometimes seems as though it's all there is to do. But what if it isn't? What if I can do something else? What happens then?"

"What do you want to do instead?"

Burt looked out of the torchlight into the dark corners of the building. He took a deep breath. When he had finished coughing he said: "Count things. I want to try counting

7

things."

"My word," said Bill, "that's a bit out of the blue. Where has this come from?"

"Well, I've been thinking and the way I see it there's only really two types of work in the world. There's moving things and counting things. And I don't really like moving things, so I'd like to try my hand at counting things."

Bill thought for a moment. "I don't think that's a good idea."

"Why not?"

"Because you're too good at moving things."

"I am?"

"Yes! You're the best. There's no-one else that can move things like you. A lot of people move things too slowly, and if you move things too slowly they rot."

"Most of these things are rotting already," said Burt. He kicked a pile of things on the floor. It was rotting and it fell apart.

"Alright," said Bill, "rot more then. But I don't have that problem with you. You're the best."

"You're just saying that, so I keep moving things."

"No I'm not," said Bill. "And besides. It's all very well wanting to start counting things, but do you have the necessary people management skills? I mean that's certainly a consideration. Managing people. Because if you want to start counting things the actual counting is only the half of it. You also have to be able to manage people who move things."

"Like you do, you mean? When you tell me what to do?"

"I'm not sure that's quite all I do. But yes."

"Because I certainly think I could tell you what to do."

"Maybe so," said Bill, "but flip that for a minute."

"I'm sorry?"

"Flip that for a minute. Ask yourself what people would think if you stopped moving things."

"I'm sorry?"

"If you stopped moving things," said Bill, "and started counting things, they'd think you were unhappy."

"I am unhappy."

"OK. But they'd think you were unhappy because I'd *managed* you badly."

"Who on earth would make that association?" said Burt.

"I would," said Bill, "that's who. And it would do incalculable damage to my self-esteem to think that the best mover of things – the best, mind you – had decided he'd rather count things because of the way I'd managed him."

"You're just saying that, so I keep on moving things."

"No I'm not," said Bill. "And besides. How do you know you'd be any good at counting things? It's more difficult than it looks, you know."

"Oh that wouldn't be a problem," said Burt, "Look: there's one, two . . ." he kicked a pile of things on the floor; it was rotting and it fell apart, ". . . two and a half, three, three and a half. See?"

"Hmm." Bill thought for a moment. The conversation wasn't turning out the way he wanted. "That's all very well, but I think we're beating around the bush here. I think the real question is not whether you'd be able to manage people or count things but whether you'd *enjoy* counting things. That's the real question. And I don't think you would, not once the novelty had worn off. There's a lot of responsibility to counting things. You'd probably hate it. In fact, I'm sure of that. You'd definitely hate it."

"Are you sure you're not just saying that, so I keep on moving things?"

"Of course not. And besides. If you were to count things, who would move them? I can't, that's for sure."

"So what do you suggest then?" said Burt. "How am I supposed to get through this crisis I'm going through, this newly-found hatred of moving things?"

"Oh, that's an easy one," said Bill. "You imagine Sisyphus happy. We must both imagine Sisyphus happy."

"That's your answer to everything," said Burt, waving his arms in exasperation, "but I am Sisyphus and I can't simply imagine myself happy. In fact, the opposite is true. When I imagine myself, I imagine myself unhappy. Because I am unhappy. Dammit Bill, I think I deserve a shot at counting things, that's all. That's all I want. A shot."

"I like your attitude," said Bill, "but I really don't think counting things is right for you."

"You're just saying that, so I keep moving things."

"No, I'm not. And besides . . ."

"And will you please stop saying 'besides'!"

"Why?"

"Because there is no besides, is there?" said Burt. "There's no besides at all. Look around you. Look at it. There's this. That's all there is. This."

10

"In that case," said Bill, "I'm not sure I understand why you think you'd be happier counting things."

Burt sighed. He had to admit that Bill had a point. He kicked something on the floor. It was rotting and it fell apart.

# HOLIDAYING IN THE MALDIVES

Before they had to close the airport, we used to go every year. Fuvahmulah was where we stayed. Yes, that's right. Well, nearly – it's Foo-*va*-moo-lah. The emphasis is on the second syllable, or at least that's what the locals told us – maybe they were having us on?! Anyway, it was beautiful, just beautiful. When we first went it was totally unspoiled, I mean there was hardly anything there. We must have gone every year for about ten years. We'd fly in and then take a taxi. That's right, the airport was in the south east, which meant we had to go the whole length of the island. The drive would take you through these groves of mango trees – just beautiful – and then you'd be in the middle of the jungle. There was this wet, tropical heat – a bit like the tropical house at the Botanical Gardens, that sort of humidity – but you got used to that after a while. And I mean the jungle was amazing, it looked like something by Rousseau, you know, with the tigers. When we first started going, the road         much more than a dirt track but that was part of its charm, I think, it really set you up for the rest of your holiday.

We stayed just off this beach on the north coast. Thoondu it was called. It was right at the edge of these massive fields of watermelons. There weren't many Brits there at all, which         really nice, but the main reason we liked it so much was because     this festival. It takes place every year, in this little sheltered bay. The last time we were there we noticed there was more development, you know, but it was still secluded and quiet. For some reason, something to do with the tides or the winds you get at the end of the monsoon, I forget which now, there was this annual...coming together? of hundreds of flying fish. Literally hundreds    them, so many that you could catch them with your hands. So what    locals would do was wade out and stand in the sea    take them out of the air. Honestly, that is all you had to do — stand in the sea and hold your hands out. I know! I know! It    amazing. It's only when you see it that you can understand what    sea means to the community. I think they felt this immense joy at being a part of the cycles of the natural world you know, part of something that was timeless, a ritual that's been carried out for centuries, even thousands of years.

I imagine it's been    more complex recently of course. Yes, that's right. With the sea level rising. The last time were there they'd started building flood defences but you have    wonder how effective they were going to be, I mean    the Indian Ocean, isn't it? Having said that, they're so resilient out    — I mean they get by    hardly anything in the way of material possessions — I think they'll find a way to adjust. It's just a shame
the airport's had to close. I know people    that tourism was part of the problem, and I can see where they're coming from, but it's also part of the solution,    it? It has to be. I mean you can't take away that level    income and    get by, however adaptable you are.

no way they're going    to reopen it either, not where it is.    the most sensible solution would be to    it inland. I'm not sure    suitable, there's a lot of land    undeveloped    it's only an airstrip, I mean    wouldn't be causing    major damage, you know?    up to them,    I suppose.

# THE STATE OF US

Even    we've effectively paid for                    to do.

relationship          sea          the sea
          life.

## WHEN HELEN LEVITT MET VIVIAN MAIER

...you see, I'm not sure it's as simple as that. Although it is true that we might have certain natural advantages. I think one of the things you have to be able to do is – now what's the best way of saying this? – be fully present in a scene –to inhabit the moment, if you like – and, at the same time, to absent yourself, so that none of you encroaches into the frame. Now you'll hear people talking about this as though it's difficult to get right, but I don't think it is, not really. It's just what we do, isn't it? Most of us anyway. It's what's expected of us, how we're supposed to be, there but not there, not there but there. Us women, I mean, not us photographers.

Having said that, we do have to make some adjustments. I'll always remember something Walker Evans used to say to me, when I was just starting out. He had a way with words did Walker, and this was obviously something he'd thought about. He said to me – and I'll never forget this – "you have to stare." By that he meant that although there were other ways of looking at what you'd decided to photograph – a child playing tag, say, or two people having an argument, or a policeman moving someone on – although you could glance or peek or pretend to be looking at something else, if you're going to train the eye, to properly train the eye, to make sure it sees what it needs to see in any scene, you have to be able to stare. And I mean literally stare. And I struggled with that at first because we aren't supposed to look at people like that. We're supposed to be looked at, to be the subject of a person's attention, a mere object of regard if you like. Not the ones doing the regarding. If you're a woman and you stare, people think you're crazy.

17

I can tell you a story about that, actually: something happened to me a few years ago. In fact, I can tell you exactly when. It was '51. I remember that because it was one of the last times I used my old Standard. Do you remember what I said about my old Standard? Anyway I was going down to Spanish Harlem a lot that summer, but I'd also started poking around the Lower East Side. I don't know if you know it? Do you know the square down there? It's got a circular stone fountain in it...begins with an 'S'...oh, what's it called?... Yes, yes that's it. Straus Square. I'd start at Straus Square then head up Canal, or north along Essex. Essex was my favourite. There was just so much going on down there, so much movement, it was just good for all kinds of shots. I remember there was a paint shop near the square – it's probably still there – Schames it was called, and it had an enormous sign for Dutch Boy Paints, with this little boy with long bright yellow hair and matching clogs. Every time I saw that it put a little spring in my step, you know? Just up from Schames there were tenements, then there was the market, on the corner of Delancey I think it was, and the Good Samaritan's Dispensary that took up a whole block. Further along were liquor stores and pickle shops and hardware stores, racks of clothing and carpets on the sidewalk, fruit and veg carts. The light seemed to change every hundred yards or so, particularly in the summer? There must have been something about the arrangement of the buildings – or the building sites! – but more than that I think it was the people that made it special. You'd see Chinese tailors and well-to-do Jewish women with these angular hats, and big, strong women from Armenia who worked in the factories, there'd be Russians and Poles and blacks, people selling watermelon, panhandlers, street performers. Everywhere you looked there were the most brilliant surprises. And the best thing was, although there

18

seemed to be no order to it, you could see it if you stared, this strange sense of everything being in its place, exactly where it belonged, however crazy it might have looked at first.

Not that it was always that easy of course. This one day — it was very hot, so it must have been around August — I was walking around Essex and I wasn't seeing anything. Although there was the usual commotion there was nothing quite coming together, and I was wondering what I should do, whether I should carry on. You have days like that, and there's not a lot you can do about it. Because if you keep going, you run the risk of trying to force things into a scene, and when you do that you end up drawing attention to yourself and that's no good because then you become conscious of being a woman on her own, on the street. Staring. Looking crazy. And as soon as that happens you're not going to take anything worth taking because you can't remove yourself from the frame. Plus it's not a good idea. I mean it's not as bad as people make out down there, certainly not in the middle of the day, but still, there are all sorts of reasons you don't want to be drawing attention to yourself on the Lower East Side.

Anyway, that was the way I was feeling. I wasn't having a good day. And then, through the crowd, through this bustling mass of everyday surprises, I saw a girl buying soda from a cart on the corner of Essex and Canal. She was wearing a pale yellow dress, lemon yellow, and one of those wide-brimmed hats, that look like they're made of straw but aren't. Very respectable. She had the most queer features, I mean the most distinctive nose, but that wasn't what stopped me in my tracks. No, it's the way she looked at me. I recognised it as my stare, you see, even though I had never seen it, I mean I could tell straight away what she was doing there. Sure enough, after I met her eye I saw she had a camera, hanging at her hip. Not only that but it was a Rolleiflex – I'd know a Rolleiflex anywhere – so she wasn't your average shutterbug either. So I stared back. I had to. I couldn't help myself. And there we were, looking at each other, barely ten feet apart, in the middle of all this noise and distraction, and it all seemed to stop. It was like there was something between us, something that was very... potent somehow. As if we knew each other, like we were old friends, and we belonged in that exact moment, in that exact place, doing what we were doing. Staring.

And that's not all. The strangest thing was, after we'd stood there for what seemed to be an age, she smiled, picked up her camera and made as if to photograph me. So I did the same. Now we're looking at each other through our lenses, pointing cameras at each other, stock still and smiling, ready to go. But for some reason I didn't take the shot. Even after all that, I didn't take the shot. And I don't know why, I mean to this day I have no idea why I didn't take a picture of this woman, this fellow crazy, this fellow starer, whoever she was.

I often think about it though, wonder how it would have turned out if I had pressed the button. Because when she walked away – and this is something else I remember clearly – I carried on up Essex and had just the best day. I know! I know! That's a strange way to put it but it's true. One minute I was having a bad time and the next I was walking along the street feeling like a million dollars. There was no reason either, I mean it must have been connected to what had happened somehow, and god knows I've thought about it, but I couldn't tell you what it was or why. All I know is, I had the absolute best day...

## PULLING TOGETHER

Laburnum Avenue was an unremarkable suburban street where the bins were emptied on time. Yasmin and Josef felt at home there until the form from the *Be a Better Neighbour!* campaign arrived.

Yasmin read the form sitting in the front room drinking tea made, as usual, with a cardamom pod. "I'm not sure about this," she said.

"Why not?" said Josef.

"It says here we've got to fill it in so we can vote and have access to healthcare."

"What's wrong with that?"

"We can already vote and we already have access to healthcare. Besides, the questions are a bit strange. Look — here's one about how often we clean our windows: 'a) Every day b) Every week or c) Other (please explain).' And here's one about deck shoes: 'Do your deck shoes have tassels?' What are tasselled deck shoes? And why is that significant?"

"I don't know," said Josef, "but I think Derek might have a pair. Do you want me to ask him?"

Derek lived across the road and, as Yasmin considered her reply, she looked out of the window and caught sight of him in the front room of his house. She waved and he waved back.

"If you think it will help."

*

A week later, as Yasmin drank her first tea of the morning, Josef asked if she'd thought any more about filling in the form, "because Derek told me if we don't we'll be liable to a fine."

Yasmin frowned. Over the course of the week Josef had resisted her attempts to discuss the form with him and she found his insistence that they should fill it in now puzzling. It suggested a passivity that was at odds with his usual gumption: why, just last year he had taken to task an assistant at The National Heritage Museum when he'd objected to the shape of Yasmin's hat. She also struggled to see what their predicament had to do with Derek. She and Josef had lived on Laburnum Avenue for ten years and it was only since the start of the *Be A Better Neighbour!* campaign that he had taken the slightest notice of either of them.

Yasmin shook her head. "I'd have thought that was all the more reason not to."

"Why? It's not as if we have anything to hide."

"Maybe. But don't you remember what happened to your grandparents after they filled in a form like this?"

"Oh please. It's not the same thing at all. That was years ago. I really do think you're overreacting."

Yasmin's puzzlement deepened. Could Josef mean what he was saying? She hoped not. Turning away from her partner, she glanced out of the window. Standing outside his house, looking at her from across the road, was Derek. She waved and, after hesitating for a moment, he waved back.

*

A week later, Josef interrupted Yasmin's tea drinking to tell her that they had wasted enough time and should fill in the

22

form without further delay. "I spoke to Derek and he said everyone on the avenue felt very strongly about it. If we don't, it will look as though we're not part of the community."

"But we are part of the community. I wave at him all the time."

"That's as maybe. But we have some fences to mend, some bridges to build."

"What do you mean?"

"He knows, Yasmin."

"Knows what?"

"How you make your tea."

"How does he know that?"

"I'm not sure. Although his windows *are* very clean. But either way I think he's right. I mean we like it here, don't we? Why put all that at risk?"

"How are we going to put that at risk by not filling in the form?"

"Didn't you see? It was in the last *Better Neighbour News!* Some people up the road who drink tea like yours didn't fill the form in. And they were... Well. It wasn't very nice, that's all."

Aha! So that was it! Yasmin tried to catch Josef's eye but he had turned away and bowed his head. At that moment, her attention was taken by someone peering in through their front room window. Derek. She hesitated and then waved, as he ducked out of sight.

Yasmin sighed.

# A MODERN HISTORY OF THE LEVANT

The path took the men along a cliff edge overlooking the sea. It rose and fell and rose again, winding through dry yellow earth. It was too hot to be walking so far and the men were sweaty and limping. They came across an outcrop of rock, shaded by a solitary fig tree. The first man said, *shall we take five?* and, slipping out of his pack, rested himself against the tree. His companion followed suit and the two of them sat shoulder to shoulder and looked out across the deep green water, to the hazy curve of the horizon.

The men wiped their brows with their sleeves.

"Sheesh, it's hot," said the second man and the first man said:

"Got that right."

"Do you reckon it's hotter than that place last year?"

"Which one?"

"The city on the river. With the date palms."

"I don't know."

"Me neither," said the second man, "I mean that was wet heat. This is dry heat. Like the desert with the ants."

"The desert with the ants?"

"Yeah. Do you remember? There was the desert with the camels and the desert with the ants. Enormous things. Red heads. The ants I mean, not the camels."

"I don't remember the ants."

"Why would you?" said the second man, and he smiled, "It wasn't your ankle they took a liking to."

"People remember different things," said the first man.

The two men took a sip of water from a bottle they passed between them. Down below there was a ship, cutting grey and shark-like through the sea. "I'm hungry," said the first man.

"Me too," said the second man. "Could do with some of that goat. I'd kill for some of that goat."

"Yeah," said the first man.

"It was good wasn't it?" said the second man.

They sipped at their water. The second man shook his head.

"Will you listen to us? Talking about eating goat, like it's no big deal. Can you imagine if we hadn't been doing this, all this time. Shoney's, that's what we'd be talking about. Whereas now we're talking about goat."

A long way overhead a jet soared, like a gull on currents of air. The second man followed its path. "I mean it's funny isn't it? We've had some crazy times, man, I've taken some crazy photographs – that woman on the back of the motorbike, the piles of fruit in that market. The hats at that wedding – sheesh! –"

" – I've seen your crazy photographs –"

" – but I think it's the food that's going to stick with me. The goat. What was that thing last summer? Was it sheep? And the rabbit! Man, that rabbit."

"The rabbit?"

"Yeah. Now that was something else."

The first man frowned. "I don't remember the rabbit."

"You don't remember the rabbit either?" said the second man. "Oh come on, you must remember the rabbit. We had it just outside that town on the coast. There was a square, with a fountain, lions on it. An old man sold you a cigarette. You must remember that. Don't you..."

The second man's voice tailed off. The first man stood up and looked up at the sky. It was impossibly blue. "There was a school," he said.

"I know," said the second man.

"A school."

"I know," said the second man, "I'm sorry."

He got slowly to his feet, patted the first man on his shoulder. The first man flinched. He bowed his head. "Assholes," he said and he punched the trunk of the fig tree. "Assholes," he said, and he punched the tree again – "assholes! ASSHOLES!" – shouting the word now, punching the tree again and again, and he kept on punching the tree until his hand was useless, a grotesque, distorted and bloody mess of flesh, torn skin and bone, until the yellow earth was spattered with dark splashes of blood.

# RUCKUS AT THE DOG AND DUCK

Last night there was a fight between two groups of Johnnie Bodens down the Dog and Duck. They'd been drinking craft beer and estate-bottled rioja in the corner of the pub. At first they'd got on, indulging in consensual bonhomie about Black Lives Matter and Vladimir Putin, the refugee crisis and membership of the EU, then someone mentioned umami and the atmosphere turned. Before long there were disagreements about salting aubergines and griddle pans and egg foo yung; when someone raised de-veining prawns, flush-cheeked acrimony slipped into visceral anger. No-one is sure now what the catalyst for the violence was – it might have been oxtail, it might have been nam pla, most likely it was cobblers – but, within minutes, the pub was rent with the sound of breaking glass, with tribal cries of "cap-o-*nata*!" and the chilling response, "Sous vide! Sous vide! Sous vide!"

## ON THE INTERNATIONAL SPACE STATION

Houston, Station – Good Morning!

Good Morning? Hello? Houston? Hello. Hello? Houston? Hous…

Ah. Hold on, let's see if this helps…

Houston are you there? No? No. OK. No, that's OK. I appreciate this is a difficult time. I'll try again later.

\*

Houston, Station. Houston? OK, still no joy. I thought I'd try again but by the looks of things, Ku-Band's down, so I'll leave it for now.

\*

Houston, Station. So this is audio only and I'm getting nothing back but that's OK – there doesn't seem to be anything wrong with the EPS and I'm guessing you're in quiescent operations mode – so I'm going to carry on anyway.

I just wanted to say that I'm good. Well, I'm doing OK, all things considered. I thought you should know that. I mean it has been a bit crazy, I won't lie to you, partly because I don't actually know what the situation is down there. I've seen a lot of cloud recently. A lot. Have you noticed it too? You must have, I guess. I mean I've seen a lot of cloud before, but never quite this much. But then it might be fine, I don't know, that's the point, isn't it? It's crazy isn't it, this situation? Whatever's going on, you must know that too. I mean you've

31

probably got a better idea than I have eh?

But I'm doing OK. I mean this isn't a million miles away from some of the scenarios in HERA, so it's not completely unprecedented. I mean obviously it's completely unprecedented but I was prepared. Sort of, at least.

OK. That's all for now. I'm good.

OK.

*

Houston, Station. So, to business. It's been a while – two days? – but I'm pretty sure I've been in some sort of shock. Now I'm getting there, working this thing out, and I think I'm ready to tell you what I'm doing, why I'm here. Why I'm *still* here. And what I plan to do. Oh, and to give you all my thanks too.

Right, so, first things first. Why I didn't go back down with Oleg and Matsushita. I know Behavioural Health might have their own ideas about this, but I want you to know it's not a decision I took lightly. I was actually thinking about it for a long time, because I'm not an impulsive person. Never have been. Oleg always jokes – always *joked* – about the time it takes me to decide anything – but then you probably knew that already. The thing is, we'd been watching what was going on – while we still had Twitter in any case – and we'd known for some time the way things were going, so when we saw the missiles on CNN and RTR and we could see it wasn't deescalating, we knew it was only a matter of time before we were told to go back down. Not to mention the 'unprecedented developments', of course. When we heard that we had some fun guessing what they might be, before we saw it wasn't funny after all. The point is, we knew what was likely to happen, so I wasn't acting on a whim. I'm not acting on a whim. I mean there's a lot of hypotheticals involved, but I have thought this through, I've been thinking about it for a long time.

Even so, I'm not going to lie to you. It was rather sudden. When the shuttle arrived, I mean, when it actually docked. That was a crazy time, for sure. I think Oleg and Matsushita thought I'd change my mind and go back down with them. Actually, that's not true – they were trying their best to *make* me change my mind. Matsushita told me he understood if I was worried about the flight, as Houston and TsUP weren't talking, though I don't know where he got that from. Oleg said I wouldn't last a week. He even asked if I was alright, if I'd had some sort of episode, which was understandable, I suppose, but given I've always been – now how can I put this? – the *steadiest* of us, he was never going to convince me, not really.

So why did I decide to stay? Well, put it like this. Even if the mission is over, people need to know that this place is still up-and-running. Still doing what it's supposed to do. Still operational. That's the long and the short of it. Because this station represents the best of us. I truly believe that. I mean we've just celebrated two years of the mission, haven't we, but we could have celebrated every single day we've been up here, because everything connected to this station is a miracle. I mean that, I absolutely do. I think we're creating a better future for all of us and I also think we're setting an example of the best of being human, of humans working together, of our potential. *Learning, Believing, Achieving, Succeeding*, you know the mantra. I mean I know that's outreach-speak but do you know what? I'll take outreach-speak at the moment, because I reckon whatever's going on down there, whatever has gone on since we last spoke, we need to know we can come out the other side. We have to believe that, we have to keep going, we have to have something to keep going *for*.

And you feel the same too, you believe that this is still worth doing. I know you do. For sure. I know you will do, John – are you there John? I hope so! – and you, Christine, and you, Brad. And… let's think. Jose! How's it going, Jose? And, Karen, of course, I'm going to assume you're still there, Karen. I mean there's not a chance you'd have thought for one minute about giving it all up, is there? I mean, I remember what happened in Saint Hubert when you had the flu and you couldn't even get out of bed, you had a temperature of 102, and you were still arguing about the content of the modules, do you remember? Fluid Science I think it was. So yeah, I know what the programme means to you. And it means the same to me. Oleg and Matsushita too. I don't care what they say, the only reason they went back down was because of Galina and Nori. If it wasn't for that, they'd still be here, just like if any of you were in my position, you'd still be here.

I mean, I know it won't be easy. Yesterday I went all over Zvesda, Colombus and Kibo, to reorient myself, try to put it into perspective. Keeping this thing operational is going to be full-time job, especially if Ku-Band's down and I'm not going to be having any DPCs or talking to the SPARTAN guys. Or, come to think of it, getting any debris reports – is the SSN still there? I mean you must be, for sure, but how do I know? So yes. Although I told him to nize it, Oleg might be right, I might not last a week, or much longer, eh. But then I'm adaptable, you know that, you all know that. Besides which, it's always been difficult. We sometimes forget that amongst the miracles. And that's never bothered me. Never bothered any of you either, has it? We've just gotten on with it, because it's what we all do, eh? We persevere. Do what needs to be done to keep his place running.

So that's where we are. I know I've been rambling a bit, but I thought you'd like to know the thinking behind my decision not to go back down. It's the least you deserve. Because we all know I couldn't do any of this without you there. So thank you. All of you. Thank you.

On which note, to business. Operations. We've still got, what? nearly 400 experiments to complete, and realistically I'm not going to finish them all, so I'm focussing on what I can keep on top of. Which means, in short, I'm all over Code S and Code M, less so Code Y. For example – let's see here, oh yes, here we are, I knew I had a list here somewhere – all of these are going to be OK: AgCam, AMS-2 and HARP. ISAAC and Meteor will keep going. NICER too and... yes, BTN Neutron. Oh and of course I'll look after SAGE III. I mean,, at some point, I'm going to audit what's still running, but for now I just wanted to give you a projection.

I've also started an audit of the food. And the good news is I've got plenty. Oleg's left the most. There's goulash, jellied pike, dried beef, borscht, mashed potatoes, buckwheat and grape juice. There's Matsushita's JAXA too, of course, and noodles, lots of noodles. And, although I haven't looked yet, I'm sure Franco and Jasmin left some packs behind. There's nothing fresh at the moment, but then I guess you knew that. I think I'll cope. I mean I'm going to miss it but I do have other things on my mind just now. Ha. The only problem is I've run out of coffee and can't seem to find any more, so that means no coffee which, as anyone who knows me will know, is bad.

Which brings me to household chores. Again, I can't do everything, but they seem to be going alright. Yesterday – ah, bear with me, was it yesterday? – yes, that's right, yesterday I had to patch-up the rotor on one of the microgravity centrifuges. That went well. And I've also cleaned the aquarium and fixed the toilet. I don't get as much done as I'd like, but by and large things have been going OK. On the flip side, there's EVAs. At the moment I'm monitoring one of the MBSU's. It's not happy, for sure. The thing is, we've had problems with this before but we've fixed it with an EVA and that's not going to happen this time, so we'll have to see how it develops.

Right, so, anyway, I think that's it for now. I'm sorry if that was a long one eh, but there was a lot of ground to cover. Oh no, wait! Are you there Mac? I hope so. You'll be glad to hear – and you're not going to believe this! – for some reason, I'm spending more time in the gym. On which note...

*

Houston, Station. I just wanted to check in to ask about the STEM Engagement guidelines. I don't know if that last one was acceptable? At the moment, I mean. Sorry!

*

Houston, Station. Quick update for you. I've just had a go at the MinION. Seemed to go OK. Will keep you posted. Oh, and I had an hour on the bike too.

Houston, Station. It's me again. I wasn't going to share this with you but I've changed my mind. This one's a bit more personal, so apologies if it's inappropriate in any way. I've made another list. You know what I'm like with lists, right? Anyway, I thought I'd do another one, as a sort of, oh I don't know, mission statement? No that's not right. The mission is still the mission eh. An objective then. Yes that's it, a performance objective. Ha! It was... how do I put this? OK, it was going to be a list of ice cream. Flavours I was going to work my way through at Summer's, when I got back. For those of you who don't know Summer's, Oleg can put you in the picture, I've bored him about it often enough. Summer's is a Toronto institution, I mean a lot of people will say Greg's is the place but Summer's has really got it going on, and I've been craving their black cherry ripple for a while now. So that was what I was going to make a list of. Summer's ice creams. But then I didn't because, frankly, I can do better than that. So what I've done is made a list of cities where I have spoken or read, cities I have presented papers in. Now there's a few of these, because my research was original and, believe it or not, I knew how to work a crowd. Ha! I know. Anyway, here's the list, these are the places. There's: London; Edinburgh; New York; Boston; Los Angeles; Washington; Quebec; Paris; Frankfurt; Amsterdam; Brussels, Madrid, Wellington, New Delhi, Sydney, Tokyo.

And then, on the other side, I thought I'd put down some places I haven't been to, but would like to. Places I'd like to read, or talk in. There's: Rostov-on-Don – thanks Oleg! – Moscow; St Petersburg; Vladivostok; Lagos; Buenos Aires; Cape Town; Rome; Barcelona; Beijing; Cairo; Berlin; Mexico City.

It's not an exhaustive list, of course, but these are the cities I've got a hankering for. I thought I'd share it with you because to me, it's a positive thing, I mean I don't know if Behavioural Health are there but I thought it might reassure you about my state of mind. Because one day, when I'm ready, or when you are, you'll send the shuttle up again and I'll go back down. One day I'll read in these cities too.

OK?

*

Houston, Station. So that's an hour-and-a-half on the treadmill and bike. I think this might be my new schedule. It's less than I've been doing but I've got more work to do, so it works out OK. You got that, Mac?

*

Houston, Station! Good morning! Right. I have some news. One of the Work Station Screens has stopped working and I don't know why. The thing is, although the other two seem fine, part of me doesn't care if they stop working too. I don't mean I've given up, far from it. It's just that I've recently acquired a slightly different perspective on things.

Ha. Go figure.

The funny thing is, I can put my finger on exactly when it happened. It was yesterday. I was in the cupola, looking out into what might as well be eternity, when I saw the Large Magellanic Cloud. You'll know about that. I first learnt about it way back, even before Chapman, I think. Yes, come to think of it I can remember boring Phoebe about it, I told you about Phoebe didn't I? Maybe not. Anyway, as I was sitting there, this figure came into my head: 163 light years. Because, of course, that's how far away it is. But the thing is, when I thought about it yesterday – that figure, that exact figure – it cheered me up no end. And I'll tell you why.

The figure didn't matter. That 163. I know it used to. I know when we learnt it, we referred to it all the time, applied it to other areas of our studies, our training, put it into context. But the context has changed. Now what matters is just the *presence* of the cloud. It being there, that's all. And this, I think, is what cheered me up. Because it puts a different slant on what I said before. I mean I had been feeling guilty about what I wasn't getting done, about not being able to keep on top of everything we had running here, but now I've realised it's less the mission as it was – data-driven, operations-led, the *detail* of it all – that matters. It's more the fact we're still here. Part of the cosmos, along with the cloud. That's what's important now.

I mean I'm right, aren't I? Think about it. I am.

Oh. Still no coffee though. And coffee is both, I mean coffee is symbol and detail, for sure. So send coffee! Ha.

*

Hello again. Nearly two hours exercise today but I think the ARED might be broken. Cranking lever's a bit stiff. Oh, and the toilet. Again. Looks like a build-up of calcium this time. Though I can fix that.

*

Houston, Station. Me again. No, really! Ha! Just a quick one. I think I've got myself a hobby. It's walking the robotic arm.

You know how the arm moves end-over-end, in this looping motion, like this? Well, it's been commented on before, but it's just like a caterpillar. Look. It clasps, like this, with its front legs and draws up its rear end, and then goes again. Isn't that mesmerising? I've always loved watching it but have never really had the time to look at it quite like this, because it's supposed to support EVAs or the shuttle docking and I've always had other things to do. But there's none of that going on at the moment, so I've been playing, moving the arm up and down the length of the station and watching it go on. Looping. Just looping.

So yeah. That's a hobby, I guess.

*

Houston, Station. Two and half hours exercise. Pushed it today. Ha!

*

Houston, Station. Another quick update. So, for those of you that didn't know, there are three hundred ants in the Biolab. Except that's not strictly true. There *were* three hundred ants in the Biolab. We were looking at how they coped in zero gravity, how this affected their interactions with other ants and if I'm telling the truth – and I don't want to upset anyone down there – I never fully understood the point of the experiment. I mean don't get me wrong, I get the fish, but I've never been sure about the ants. And so yes, I know this is potentially very bad, but I've just let them out.

I had this idea, you see. I don't know why, but it made perfect sense at the time. I let them go and then I made sure they all came together, so they were floating in a cloud. Then I secured my feet and moved my hands through the cloud, like this, really gently, feeling these creatures on the skin of my hands, the touch of hundreds of tiny insects, and as well as touching living things it was like I was touching life itself, you know? and it was all a little bit overwhelming because I don't get many opportunities like that, and I felt this crazy sort of, oh I don't know, almost *elation*.

So yeah. All this going on and here's me, communing with ants. Ha.

\*

The funny thing is, I've just remembered the old cliché about how ants will be one of the few things to survive a nuclear war, and it made me laugh. But it's not very funny is it?

\*

Two hours exercise. Mainly on the bike. Though I have fixed the ARED.

\*

Houston, Station. Hello again. It's been a while, hasn't it? I'm sorry about that. The thing is, everything's been positive up until now, hasn't it, mostly at any rate. I mean I was a bit shocked at first, for sure, but I've been trying hard to stay upbeat. I've meant what I've said too, don't get me wrong, but I think it's beginning to sink in. What's gone on here. Or what might have gone on. Or  – and this is the thing – what *may as well* have gone on. Whatever, now I've started to process it – I mean properly process it – I'm angry. Really angry. And it's affecting everything I do. Everything.

I thought about this the other day. I have this poem, that I read as often as I can. It's called *Cycle of Community* and it's by someone called Margaret Avison. And the last line, it goes 'we half hear the foghorn and remember the lake, and night', and it's always seemed, oh I don't know, comforting, in a way. It connected me to home. And not just because we're both from Toronto, either, I mean that's something you learn up here: I'm from T Dot, Oleg is from Rostov-on-Don, Matsushita is from Yokahama, but these distinctions don't exist, not when you're looking down at the earth. For me, that's what the poem is about, that sense of belonging, not to *place* but to community. To humankind, if you like, if you want to put it like that. But when I read it the other day, it just came across as sentimental nonsense because no-one thinks like that anymore. If they did we wouldn't be in this situation, would we? And that makes me sad but it makes me angry too.

I've also I've realised this station is too big for one person to run on their own. I just can't do it. Not for as long as I'd like to anyway, however long that might be. I mean I'll keep going, of course I will, I'll go on for as long as I can – I've got to, haven't I? – but I shouldn't still be here, not really, not on my own. Playing out these scenarios in my head that just don't compute, that don't make any sense – or *shouldn't* make any sense – turning them over and over. I shouldn't have had to do what I've done. Do you know what I mean?

I mean what *am* I doing here? I stayed because I thought I had a job to do, because I didn't think you should take this station out of the equation, because what I was doing was still – in a strange way – a part of what was going on, and that we needed reminding – no, no, let's get this right, you people down there needed reminding – that we could be better than cancelled missions and emergency evacuations, better than whatever the hell is actually happening. I thought that despite it all we were still in this together. But do you know what? It doesn't feel like that anymore. I don't feel a part of what's going on at all.

Put it this way. Would I notice if something down there had just ceased to exist? Like a city? Or a civilisation? Or love? Jesus. What would happen? Would there be signs? Clues? You tell me. Is it the clouds, is that it, are the clouds a sign? There is still a lot of cloud around, is that it? Or... or is it the lights? Would the lights go out? And if so, how? I mean I can't see them at the moment anyway, but would they all go out at the same time, or one-by-one? Or would none of that happen? Would the end of us be like the death of a person I never knew, something that was too inconsequential or too profound to register?

So yeah. I'm too far removed to be involved. And being put in that position makes me angry. And that doesn't feel good. So I'm not sleeping properly. When I'm asleep I'm having these dreams, these crazy dreams. Last night I dreamt of the patterns that people make on the surface of the earth – I used to talk about them with Matsushita – the lights of conurbations and the deltas of rivers lit up like connections in the brain, like neural networks or open clusters of stars. Then I dreamt of explosions, time-lapse flowers opening in tiny puffs of unfurling smoke and dust, and although, yes, there was a poetry to it, and it was beautiful in a way, it was also endlessly, relentlessly terrifying. So I woke up terrified and asked myself why and then got angry all over again.

And because I'm not sleeping properly, when I'm awake, I'm falling apart. I'll be in the middle of something and

43

then I'll get a rush of images and sensations and memories. Most come together for the shortest of time but two are really vivid and keep coming back. I see Oleg, with his family, in a car on a road, travelling quickly in this strange grey light. It is snowing. Oleg's children are in good spirits, they are singing *chunga changa* – this children's verse he used to sing – but Oleg is desperate. He is trapped, there is nowhere he can go; there's this menace, this threat, oppressive, everywhere, it's in the air itself, and the air the snow is falling from is dark and foul, and it closes in, envelops the car and there's no getting away.

Then I see Phoebe. My sister. She's dead. I mean she died. She's been dead for some time. Five years. Five years? Yes. Five years. Anyway, I see her and we are having a picnic in High Park, in the garden by the lake, and the grass is brown, parched, burned by the sun but the cherry trees are in bloom, there's blossom on the cherry trees and they're beautiful, the leaves are browning but the blossom is full, and I tell Phoebe I have just been accepted for training and she toasts me with a glass of ice-cold Viognier.

Ha. First ice cream and now Viognier. Jesus Murphy.

So me and my sister talk about science – to her it was all 'science' – and she calls me a keener again – she was always calling me a keener, and I was, I guess – and asks me how condensation forms – as if I'd know! – and then we're laughing and we and lie down and look up into the sky – look up here – and drift away, like we are children again, and there's this yellow light and I feel this…contentment. And then it goes bad. Then a park ranger tells us there has been an assault and we should leave the area, and everything closes in like a typical nightmare and, all of a sudden, everything is in flux and I can't trust anyone. I can't trust Phoebe, that's

44

the main thing. I mean nothing like that ever happened to us in High Park, not all the times we went there but that's the point of falling apart I suppose. Because it has to end badly, doesn't it? Me having a dream like that, up here, just now.

And then it's like I come round and I can't tell if any of this happened or not, I mean I'm finding it difficult to know what is real anymore, and which of my memories are just sentimental poetry or bad dreams. It's like my idea of reality is going round in an endless circle.

It's the anger that's making me feel like this. It distorts everything. And I don't know. I don't know what I'm doing up here anymore. Except rambling. And if there's one thing I told myself I wouldn't do, it's ramble.

I'm sorry. I mean I am going to carry on, of course I am. I have no choice, do I? But I wanted to say that. I'm sorry. No, I'm not sorry. I'm angry. Because none of this is anything to do with me.

*

A question for you. Did it have to be like this? I mean if we could start again, build the world again, build the world from scratch, knowing what we do now, would it be different the next time around? Or is all of it, all our achievements and failures, the passing consolations we find in poetry and numbers, is all of it an inevitable consequence of our refusal to accept our irrelevance? A determination to prove that we mean something in relation to everything else, when we don't, not really. I mean god help us, not that I believe in god, but god help us.

*

Houston, Station. That's the thing though, isn't it? It might seem as though I'm losing it, but I can't be, can I? Because going insane means thinking and behaving in a manner that is disengaged from reality, and what is the reality of the situation? I know I've been talking about how we're all in this together, but what is 'this'? What are the norms of perception or, or behaviour that I am transgressing? Against what can my thoughts and actions be judged irrational? I mean I don't know, not for sure, but I can guess. And the idea is ridiculous.

*

Houston, Station. Another bad day. Or is it some more bad days? I don't know, I think I've lost count. I'm sorry.

The thing is, however much I try to dress it up as something else, this is a failure. All of it. You've failed and because of you, I have too. I mean yes, I know we fail all the time, all of us, but this failure is different. Whatever it is, wherever we are right now, I've seen enough to know that this failure is absolute. It's a failure of everything. It's obscene.

Because we're supposed to be past all this now. We're supposed to have evolved. I mean that's what this station is all about. That's what I'm doing here. To show that, somehow, we've improved. But we haven't, have we, otherwise we wouldn't here, where we are today. We're going round in circles. Ha! Like me with these comms. Looping, you know?

So yeah.

Houston, Station. Hello Houston. There's something I should clarify, something I've just realised. Or maybe I knew all along, I'm not sure. Anyway. The thing is, although I know that everything's not OK, I'm assuming that some things are as they were, and that even though you aborted the mission and Ku-Band is down, and I sometimes feel alone, and I don't know who exactly I'm talking to, I'm talking to someone at least. That whatever has gone on hasn't affected the programme, at least not terminally, and you're still there. Maybe not all of you. But most of you. Some of you.

But I might be wrong. Because there is another scenario, isn't there? The power for this place might be coming from some sort of auxiliary process that kicks in in the event of an emergency evacuation. I don't know, do I? I don't know the detail of quiescent operations mode, or what happens in crazy situations like this. And that's a little disturbing, I'm not going to lie. I mean I try not to think about it, but the possibility exists that I'm on my own, not metaphorically, or physically, but *literally*. That I'm not actually talking to anyone. That there's no-one left.

Or – and this is worse in a way – what if there are people down there but no-one's listening? If everyone *might as well* have gone? If there's no-one interested in what I'm doing, in what we used to do? We might have lost everything that made all this possible in the first place. It might just be an idea we once had, that's all.

And if there's no-one there, or no-one that's listening, if this place is being powered by some sort of auxiliary process, it means, of course, the power could go off at any moment. All of this could end in an instant. And if that's the case – bear with me here – then it follows that everything that has happened – every moment that has gone – has been leading up to the lights going out. Do you see what I mean? That there's an irresistibility to it. An inevitability. Up here, it's easy to imagine there's some sort of continual motion, that everything is in a constant state of flux, but perhaps it isn't. Maybe you only loop for so long, and then you stop. Just like that.

Ha.

I say ha.

*

Hello again. Please scratch that last one. Was just having a moment there. Reading too much into things. It's just hard, with so little to go on. So as you were. John. Christine. Jose. Oleg? Whoever.

*

Houston, Station. Just to let you know, I've been thinking about it and I might go outside. I mean I know that if I open the door, I'll have failed, just like everyone else, but at what? Yeah, tricky one that, eh?

I'm not unhappy about it. It's not a bad way to go, all things considered. Better than some of the alternatives, eh? You'll know this, or some of you will – you drown. That's all. Just drown. Set off with three litres of oxygen and slowly drown. It might actually be quite a sign-off. Think about it. It'll be me and forever, I mean I'll be free of everything except existence, with just enough time to think about, oh I don't know, ice cream and Viognier and High Park, maybe hallucinate a little bit, make peace with god knows what, and then nothing, a return to cosmic dust, to the particles we came from, home again in a way. And that'll be the end of it. No, really. An end to the ridiculousness, an end to the obscenity. An end to the irrelevance and the meaning, an end to my part in the failure, an end to the looping, an end to all of it. Just the end, you know? Because it's a lot for one person, keeping this going. It's a lot for one person to do.

Except I don't think it's what I'm doing or not doing that's the problem, not really. No. It's a lot for one person to *bear*.

I mean I haven't decided yet. But I have to admit although I'm not particularly angry or sad anymore, I'm struggling. With this, with you, with all of it.

And – and this is really strange – with Phoebe too. I'm missing Phoebe, missing her like you wouldn't know. It's been five years and I thought I'd got used to it, but I haven't, I get that now, I mean it's crazy how much I miss her, being up here, like this. How much everything comes back to that, in a way, despite it all. Everything comes back to that.

Jesus Christ. More than ever, Phoebes. I'm sorry.

I'm sorry.

And anyway. I still have no coffee. And I would kill for a coffee, literally kill. Do you hear me? Do you? Do you? Fuck it, I have no coffee. So yeah.

*

Houston, Station. I mean I probably won't actually. Open the door. I know I said I would but I probably won't. I'll probably just sit it out. I mean it doesn't make sense does it, coming all this way and then doing that?

Yeah. So. Come on. Joke's over. Open the comms.
I know you're there. Open the comms, and send me the
shuttle. I'm ready to come back down. I think the mission...
oh.

Houston?

What's that?

Houston, can you hear me?

Hello?

## THE EXPERIMENT

The woman is a university lecturer who is known for her unorthodox approach to teaching. In preparation for a forthcoming module she has devised a three-part experiment. Each morning, at about 9AM, the man she has chosen to help with the experiment leaves the Arts and Law Building where she works. She doesn't know what he does or where he is going – whether he has started work at 8 and is nipping out for a coffee, whether he is going home after a night shift, whether he actually works in the Arts and Law Building or is just passing through – but this is irrelevant; what matters is that she arrives at the building as he leaves.

On the day she intends to start the experiment, the woman checks her equipment, which consists of a tiny camera attached to her coat. At about 9AM, she arrives at the Arts and Law Building to discover her timing is perfect. As she enters the building from the campus, the man goes to leave the building's foyer. The woman and the man catch each other's eye. The man holds the door to the foyer open for her and the woman holds the door to the campus open for him. Between the external door and the door to the foyer there is a space. The space can be crossed in three seconds or a hurried second and a half, which is not enough time for the woman and the man to simultaneously let go and reach each other's door before it swings shut. A moment arrives: there is a twitch of muscle and intent. The moment passes. An opportunity is gone and the experiment begins.

"After you," says the man.

"No," says the woman, "after you."

"I insist," says the man

"I couldn't," says the woman.

"Well, we can't stand here all day," says the man.

"Oh I don't know," says the woman. "It might be fun."

The man scans the woman's voice for a recognisable tone and doesn't find one. He purses his lips and rolls his eyes. There is potential stasis. He looks from the woman to the wide open spaces of the campus over her shoulder and back again. People walk through the doors that the woman and the man hold open; the man shakes his head and the woman can see that the experiment might fail before it has properly started. But it doesn't. She holds her door open for him and he holds his open for her: there is stasis. The woman breathes a sigh of relief.

The woman says: "If we're going to be here for any length of time, we should probably sit down."

"I'm sorry?" says the man.

"On the count of three then? One... two... three..."

The woman sits down. The man tuts loudly and frowns. He shakes his head again then joins her on the floor of the space between the doors.


The woman and the man sit with their backs to the doors, holding them open. Minutes pass, an hour. The woman is calm but the man is unhappy. He admonishes himself: "this is ridiculous!" He counts to three, stands up, making sure his door doesn't swing shut. Puffs out his cheeks. "Do you know what? I've had enough of this now."

"Why?"

"It's pointless, isn't it? A waste of time."

"What makes you say that?"

"Well, what am I doing? I don't know. I don't know what I'm doing. Or why."

"Ah," says the woman, "maybe that's the point."

"But I haven't got the time for it. I've got places to be. I'm missing meetings."

"Off you go then," says the woman and the man gives her a look, then stays where he is.


More time passes. More people pass through the doors. Some stop, gathering in the foyer or outside the building. As they congregate, they are joined by others. They look at the man and woman who are sitting and then standing and then sitting in the space between the doors, holding them open. They ask questions. This is the second part of the experiment, and the woman is pleased with how it is progressing.

"What are you doing?" someone asks.

"I'm not sure," says the woman.

"Who knows?" says the man.

"Why are you here?"

"No particular reason," says the woman.

"I've no idea," says the man.

The people giggle. The woman and the man are strange. Harmless though. The people take photos, text friends. The man notices the attention he is receiving and perks up. His eyes brighten and he grins. If he is going to go viral, he might as well put on a show. He counts to three, gets to his feet, whistles and waves at the onlookers. Sings half-remembered choruses of *Don't Worry Be Happy* and *Happy Talk* and *Always Look on the Bright Side of Life* and *Happy*; says to the woman: "Now I'm going to call your bluff. You said it might be fun, so do you want to play some games?"

"If you say so," says the woman, "though I should probably tell you I'm filming you. Are you OK with that?"

"The more the merrier!" says the man. "Are you ready?"

The woman nodded.

"Onetwothree," he says and he sits down and then "Onetwothree," and he stands up and then "Onetwothree," and he's back on the floor, a little dizzy but laughing away. He is delighted to see the woman mirrors both his actions and the speed of his movements, so he says: "I've got a better idea. I Spy?" and the woman says: "Go on then." The man says: "I spy with my little eye something beginning with… 'd'," and the woman says "Door?" and the man says, "Very good!"

"My turn!" says the woman. "I spy with my little eye something beginning with 'c'."

"Chair?" says the man, pointing into the foyer of the building.

"No. I'll give you a clue. It connects you to your door."

"I give up," says the man.

"Chain," says the woman. She mimes an attempt to free his arm.

"You big cheat!" says the man. "You can't see that."

"I can," says the woman.

"Really? Very good! Did you hear that everyone? What fun!"

He laughs again, like a comedy madman. This confuses further the people watching; although they continue to film and point and muse and talk, they are unsure of the spectacle they are witnessing.

*

It is afternoon. Word has spread. More people come to look at the woman and the man holding open the doors. After his earlier exertions, the man's enthusiasm has dissipated. He is tired. The mood of the crowd has also changed. People are less inquisitive, less decorous than before. They ask no questions. Instead they point fingers, call names. They accuse the woman and the man of being pranksters, elitists, appeasers, racists, Nazis, bullies, sluts and spreaders of disease. They form cohorts, informal at first, then enforced by glares and nudges and shoves. As they point their phones, they denounce the woman and the man as apologists for this, avatars for that, flag wavers for the other. At the edge of the groups, men with beards appear; they brandish books and fill the air with spittle. There is a lot of noise. "Why can't you just leave us alone?" says the man but his contribution goes unheard in the clamour.

Not that everyone looking on is hostile. In addition to the brickbats, there are voices praising the woman and the man for their courage, their stoicism, their ingenuity. One such flatterer has a particularly inviting smile. He elbows his way to the front of the crowd, stands between the woman and the man and stretches out his arms. "You guys," he says, "you guys are awesome. I love your work. How would you like to make lots of money?" The woman tilts her head and says: "I'm not interested, thank you," and the man with the smile scowls and mutters, "Losers."

The scowling man leaves the building. So do others. Those that remain are drawn to the more obvious of the groups that are milling about. By now, some of the cohorts are louder, more persuasive than the rest and it is their voices which can be heard above the quiet, the unsure or cowed. Gradually. though, even they lose interest in the woman and the man and argue instead about the differences that have arisen amongst themselves or between each other. There is shouting and scuffles break out until – happy with their day's work – they also abandon the scene.

"Blimey!" says the man, when he and the woman are alone once again, "that was a bit much."

"And yet you're still here."

"Oh I can't go now."

"No?"

"Certainly not! If I go without you there'd be implications, wouldn't there?"

"Maybe," says the woman.

"People would draw conclusions. Most of them wrong."

"Haven't they already done that?"

"Ah, but this would be different. They'd be rubber-stamping or disproving the first wrong, wouldn't they, and that would just create another."

"Maybe," says the woman.

"There's another reason too," says the man. "I think I'm getting somewhere. Working this thing out."

"Excellent! What do you think is going on then?"

"Well I don't think it's about the here-and-now. The obvious…"

"…it rarely is…"

"…but I do have my theories."

And the woman and the man exchange smiles.

*

It is evening. The light has failed. The woman and the man are sitting on the floor leaning against the open doors of the Arts and Law building. They have been quiet for some time but although they haven't spoken directly about their wishes, they are each determined to see the night through. As they sit, the woman begins to turn over in her head the possible ramifications of her experiment, even as she wonders how it might end. The man looks past the woman into the shadows of the darkened campus. He, too, is contemplative. Then, in the distance, he sees five, six figures moving quickly towards the building. "What's this?" he says, "what's going on now?"

As the figures get nearer the man can see that they are wearing hoods and carrying sticks and planks of wood. The woman looks at them and lowers her eyes to the floor. The man is alarmed. He says: "Wait! You knew this was going to happen, didn't you?" and the woman says: "It was certainly a possibility." "But why?" says the man. "I don't understand."

The figures with sticks are closer now, running, their faces hidden; the woman raises her head quizzically, and she and the man just have time to count to three and stand up before the men are upon them and the experiment is concluded.

# THE TALE OF BIG HAL AND THE
# BETHANY TOWER

Once, in an overly typical suburb, there lived two overly typical couples. Their names were Laura and David and Richard and Sarah and they had met at the city's university while studying for Masters degrees in Psychology. The attraction between them had been instant. "There was just something about you," confided Laura to Sarah some years later, "you were our kind of people." This 'something' had endured and the two couples had been friends ever since.

The friendship was a tight-knit affair. The couples filled their twenties with the same local bands and popcorn films and prizewinning books but their compatibility was more than merely social – they saved money together too and at thirty they'd taken their first, simultaneous steps onto the property ladder. The houses they bought were a mile apart. They each had three bedrooms, kitchens made in Germany, gardens front and back. By now the foursome was meeting weekly for badminton at the nearest sports centre, fortnightly for drinks up the pub and monthly for dinner: Laura or Sarah would host while Richard or David cooked and the conversation bubbled unthreateningly, like a post-ironic fondue. So close were the couples that, when the time came for them to have children, it was no surprise that their pregnancies coincided and they gave birth – to a boy and a girl – on the very same day.

Laura and David's daughter was called Bethany and Richard and Sarah's son Henry. For the first few months parenthood suited all concerned. The babies were good-natured and distinctively beautiful – Henry had the chubbiest

59

thighs and a thick head of hair and Bethany was blessed with blue eyes and piano player's fingers – and the two couples found themselves exposed to a new and powerful love, that of mother and father for child. Such a love can be unsettling however, and so it was that, as the months passed, the two couples began to feel uneasy.

The source of their anxiety was a common one in the suburb. Once upon a time, the couples had responsibility only for their own avowedly modest hopes and expectations; now they had responsibility for their children's too. And when it came to their children, modest just wouldn't do. At first, the new parents coped easily enough. They knew that a successful child was a well-nurtured child and wasted no time in enrolling Bethany and Henry in swimming lessons, music appreciation classes, Baby's First French. They also monitored their playtimes. Gifts were vetted and the only permissible TV tie-ins were from the BBC; all were replaced before Henry or Bethany had reached the first year of the recommended age range. But a problem was looming.

Although Bethany and Henry were often in the same place at the same time, there was no such common ground to be found in their responses to the activities that had been so conscientiously laid before them. While Bethany bobbed happily in armbands, Henry preferred to sit down and splash. While she was making a decent pre-toddler stab at the Sun Salutation, he crawled off in search of the stem-ginger biscuits, while she hit drums, he shook a triangle. If Beth was an obviously bright child with an empirically verifiable twinkle in her eye, then Henry's gifts were of an altogether more intangible nature.

Initially, Laura and David's delight in their daughter's developmental progress was tempered with an awareness of their friends' predicament. "Do you know," said Laura, on Bethany's familiarity with solid food, "she's eating a whole kiwi by herself now? Would Henry like one? No? Are you sure? Oh. No, no, that's OK." With the arrival of her daughter's first word – Prius – she was quick to reassure Sarah about the absence of her son's loquacity: "Ahhh, look at him. Sitting there, holding his counsel. You can just tell he's taking it all in. Can't you?"

Similarly, when Bethany began to walk, David was very solicitous of his friend Richard. "I wouldn't worry about it if I were you. Girls just develop that bit quicker than boys. It's got nothing to do with environment. Or even diet." Richard and Sarah were also quick to play down the significance of their son's comparative lack of precocity. There were, after all, mitigating circumstances. Plenty of children were late developers and Bethany was just that little bit happier being the centre of attention than Henry. Not to mention the fact that Laura and David – bless them – were sometimes a little bit – just a little bit, mind you – *pushy*. Despite their initial equanimity however, Richard and Sarah's patience was not without bounds. On the occasion of the children's second joint birthday party, Henry met with an unfortunate accident and fouled the paddling pool at the precise moment that Laura was finishing an anecdote about a traffic jam and the preternatural nature of Bethany's bladder control. It was an unfortunate juxtaposition. And one that marked the point at which Richard and Sarah's tolerance of their friends' attitude began to pall.

"I'm not being funny", said Richard, when everyone had left, "but hasn't Laura mentioned that before?"

"Twice."

"I thought so. And don't take this the wrong way but…"

"...those two are getting on your nerves?" said Sarah. "Tell me about it. I mean I love her dearly but the way she goes on..."

The way Laura went on was OK, up to a point. Her tone may have implied a rivalry between Henry and Bethany but this was to be expected. An element of competition between children was healthy and welcome. After all, without the incentives that it brought, how could they hope to fulfil their potential? But direct comparison of children by parents was taboo, schadenfreude was verboten. There were rules governing this kind of thing – and Laura had broken them. It was obvious to Richard and Sarah that their easy-going reaction to Laura and David's challenge was being misinterpreted. Maybe even taken as a tacit admission of their son's inferiority. This was not an acceptable situation. There was a imbalance here and it needed to be redressed.

In the weeks that followed, Richard and Sarah set about trying to find something – anything – at which their son's prowess would highlight a developmental deficiency in his young friend. Their forays into this most socially delicate of tasks did not meet with immediate success. They began, eagerly enough, on the occasion of Laura and David's next visit. But their casual mention of Henry's aptitude for putting together a 12-piece jigsaw puzzle was flat-batted by their newly accredited rivals with an insouciance that served to frustrate them further. "Oh," said Laura. "Yes, that's very good. Bethany did something just like that. I forget when now."

A pattern developed. With every subsequent contact with Laura and David, Henry was encouraged to demonstrate his unusual hand-printing skills, his spooky ability to kick a ball with his left foot, his recognition of a wide variety of herbivorous dinosaurs. Yet nothing seemed to affect Laura and David's smug pride in the progress of their beloved daughter.

Soon, Richard and Sarah began to panic. While Henry slept they fretted, when he was awake they despaired. So desperate did they become, they resorted to trying to teach their two-year-old son five syllable words from books for gifted pre-teens. On one memorable occasion, Richard nearly hyperventilated when it appeared that Henry had peeled his own banana; alas, it turned out to be the handiwork of his wife.

And then, quite unexpectedly, when Richard and Sarah had given up hope and had begun to investigate the more exceptional syndromes that may be accounting for their son's unexceptional development, Henry built a tower. It wasn't much – just eight wooden blocks topped off with a Lego Espresso maker – but it was enough. It was tall, the tallest tower the boy had yet built, and he'd built a few. More importantly it was taller by far than anything of a similar design they had seen built by the blessed Bethany.

"Look!" said Sarah, the next time Laura and David dropped by, "Henry built this! All by himself! It's very good, isn't it?" Laura and David ooh-ed and ahh-ed, said nothing. They were underwhelmed by this demonstration of Henry's prowess in putting things on top of one another and perplexed by Sarah's insistence on drawing attention to it. Her exclamations however, were tinged with a desperation that they found curiously provocative. On their way home, Laura and David sat in contemplative silence. And then, without a word to each other, they ushered Bethany into their living room, presented her with a box of Duplo and the promise of a fruit-sugar treat and left her to her own carefully monitored devices.

The following weekend, Richard and Sarah turned up on Laura and David's doorstep with some exciting news. "He just keeps building it!" said Sarah to Laura, as they were shown in, "it's so tall, I don't know how it's still standing!"

"It is very impressive," agreed Richard, "I mean he's always shown an interest in engineering, but even so…" The words dried on Richard's lips. For there, in Laura and David's living room, stood David and Bethany. And the little girl was putting an abacus on top of a tower made of toys that was indisputably bigger than that of his son.

"The bloody cheek of it," said Richard to Sarah later that evening, but his words prompted no reply. What could Sarah say? The callousness of David and Laura's betrayal went deeper than either of them could express. This time, merely redressing the balance would not be enough. For now the competition had begun in earnest.

Richard and Sarah began to make their son's tower bigger, taller and wider. At first Henry helped. He was encouraged as often as he was cajoled and the activity was, after a fashion, fun. But his attention span was short and he had lost interest long before the structure outgrew him. It was then that Richard and Sarah continued to build by themselves. A mile away, David and Laura built too. "We can't let them win", said Laura and David agreed.

If each couple was utterly dedicated, they were also meticulous in their attention to detail. It wasn't enough that their tower should dwarf and belittle that of their erstwhile friends – it had to look like the work of a child, too. This was an illusion that mattered: they had their self-respect to think of, after all. And so the towers were built, as children's towers are, haphazardly. Magnetic letters of the alphabet and farmyard animals were incorporated into the structures along with draughts sets, short-tennis rackets and trains; they were held together with skipping ropes and sellotape, decorated with stickers and craft-shop glitter and wobbily buttressed with fire engines and cardboard tubes and pots of water-based paint. Despite the seemingly indiscriminate nature of their construction, the towers also morphed continuously into likenesses that could have sprung from a child's imagination: at first they resembled abstracted bunny rabbits or ducks but as they grew, they began to take on more sinister forms, those of monsters that may have crawled out from under the bed.

And grow they did. They quickly grew taller than bookcases, wider than sofas. Before long, they were too big to be contained indoors. One week, under the cover of darkness, the two couples transplanted their towers, piece by piece, into their front gardens – and still they built. Ladders and makeshift scaffolding appeared. The towers were now bigger than houses and had begun to attract the attention of neighbours and passers-by. "Lovely day for it!" they'd volunteer, as Richard or Sarah or Laura or David balanced up a ladder clutching a bucket of sand or a cookery kit, a globe or stick under their arm. But a lovely day for what?

Unaware of their genesis, no passers-by knew what the towers were, or represented. For some, their skyward striving was a sign of existential disquiet, a yearning, if not for an understanding of the cosmos and its doings, then for the meaning of life in the overly typical suburb. To others, they looked like enormous, satiric totem poles, around which people would be expected to dance, or tiptoe, in reverence or wonder or awe. There were only two points on which everyone who saw them agreed. The first was that the towers were singularly ugly constructions. The second was that they had been built with little regard for their structural integrity. They were top-heavy and bulged uncomfortably in the middle, their foundations were flimsy and they swayed in the slightest of breezes. It was almost as if – however painstakingly they had been put together – they were missing something, something fundamental to their existential wellbeing.

And all the time the towers grew, the shadows they cast lengthened. Before long, the two couples had put on hold everything that was not connected to their construction. They built in the mornings before breakfast, in the evenings through the time they used to set aside for dinner; at weekends – with breaks only to check (by drive-by) on the progress of their rivals – they built all night. So integral to the lives of the families did the structures become, they were given nicknames, Big Hal and The Bethany Tower.

Meanwhile, their namesakes suffered. Where Henry and Beth had once been paraded daily in high-end mail-order togs, now they sat, wan and alone, their noses pressed against the windows of their empty recreation rooms. Their necks got dirty. They started to watch American cartoons, eat microwaved meals. Henry's hair began to knot, Beth sucked her fingers to stumps; their houses were emptied of all playthings that could reasonably double as building materials, their weekends were no longer enlivened with visits to nearby properties in the National Trust. Instead, the neglected boy and girl were taken to charity shops, to look for any toys or games that could be pressed into service as makeshift bricks and mortar.

Once, the two couples narrowly avoided each other in the PDSA of a neighbouring suburb. "What if they twig?" said Laura, "we'd never live it down!"

"They'd think they'd won," observed Richard.

From that day on, the families went shopping only if disguised. At first they experimented with wigs, a variety of hats. They tried sombreros, toppers, the occasional fez. Gradually though, the fear of discovery drove them into ever more elaborate outfits and they were forced into wimples and tutus, ball gowns and lederhosen, cassocks and chaps; the children wore oversized shades and while Henry was incognito in a skirt, Bethany was dressed as a boy.

One day, arriving home from just such a shopping trip, Laura and David were approached by their neighbours. Laura was bearded and David wore the face-paint of a clown. They were carrying a selection of spacehoppers, for the Bethany Tower now resembled a troll and was in need of a nose. Their neighbours were inquisitive and a conversation began in the front garden of their house. While her parents were thus distracted, Bethany spotted an old panda that was embedded, like a memory, in the base of the tower that bore her name. The toy had a look about it that the little girl found attractive. The look said 'play with me' and, keen to accept the invitation, she began to tug at the panda's arm. Above her, The Bethany Tower wobbled. At that precise moment, a mile away, with Richard and Sarah similarly unmindful of his movements, Henry attempted to free a rocking horse from the foundations of Big Hal. Above him, Big Hal shuddered.

The children pulled and pulled. The toys held fast at first and were then torn free. And as their structures were fatally compromised so those two unholy towers came thundering down in a terrible cacophony of underused playthings and authentically poor design. And Henry and Bethany were crushed to death while the couples looked on, shocked, hapless, oblivious...

## TAKING BACK CONTROL

Nigel woke, as he did every day, in an inexpensive guesthouse and to the promise of a long drive. Today – if there were no developments before he left – he was travelling from Morpeth to Plymouth Hoe, a journey of some 400 miles. In many respects this was the optimum distance, necessitating only the most minor of diversions. Sometimes his destination would be closer by and he'd have to plan more significant detours, wasting half the day on roads he didn't need to travel. Once he'd struggled terribly with a nightmare trip of barely 60 miles. That morning, as he did every morning, Nigel plugged in his laptop, checked his email for overnight developments. There were none, and no new messages on his mobile either. So today was a done deal: Plymouth Hoe it was. He switched on This Morning, clipped his nose hair and took a shower.

Nigel got his information from a network of contacts he had nurtured over two decades of life on the road. For twenty years he had traversed the cities and shires of England, selling driving gloves, car coats, handbrake covers, thermos flasks and heated seat cushions. He was retired now and had nothing to sell but he had taken care to keep in touch with his former customers. Because although there were websites that supposedly offered the same intelligence, Nigel was in no hurry to announce his intentions to The Surveillance State. And Nigel had unfinished business.

He had learned things on the road. About injustice and oppression and the evils of the world. About how people were abused and exploited on a daily basis by the faceless functionaries and unaccountable officialdom of a corrupt and wasteful bureaucracy. And how, of all of the millions of people under the jackboot of the state, it was the motorist that had it worst of all. Their treatment had awakened something in him, a defiant spirit, something of Olde Englande, something of Shakespeare and Nelson and Robin Hood. Because Nigel was a motorist too and if there was one thing he would not tolerate, it was being taken for a fool by his so-called lords and masters.

By the time he was out of the shower Nigel had two messages. This was no surprise. His informants were conscientious and vigilant, their eyes on every forecourt in the land. He read the texts. The news was good. There were stirrings in the Midlands. After the Plymouth Hoe he had already pencilled in the Oadby – although it had let him down recently and he'd had to sputter on to the fall-back stop-gap in Wigston Magna – but now there was also word of a promising – if anomalous – Harborne, a fortnight hence. Before that, Penrith at 1.26, an Orpington trialling 1.257, the maverick in Bude as low as 1.246…

Nigel breakfasted, as usual, on a Full English. He replenished his thermos, put on his car coat. He put on his driving gloves and went to his car. A call came in, then another. The next few days had filled up nicely. He would stop at the garage down the road, avail himself of what he knew to be the cheapest petrol in the whole country. He would take a full tank, of course, to make sure he got every last drop of his money's worth. Then he would set off for the Plymouth Hoe, driving so as to arrive with an empty tank and ready to do it all again, to stick it to the Man, a proud Englishman standing up against the world, unbowed, unbeaten and always – always – one step ahead of the game…

## THE STATE OF US

Oh, the state of us! You want a story about the state of us? I don't know about that but I can tell you the story of a city.

The city is Birmingham and the story begins a long time past the obvious first lines. Not for me the narrative of the river Rea – oh Rea, Father Rea, to whom all Brummies pray! – nor of the settlement that emerged from its banks of Keuper sandstone some ten thousand years ago; not the market charter, nor Boulton nor Beatrice Cadbury nor the digging of canals. Rather I shall begin on 20 November 1940, on a night of earthly terror and cosmic alchemy, when Birmingham was in mortal danger and hundreds of bombs fell from the sky above the city. Many people were atomised that night, by the terrible autumnal storm. They were lovers and foundry workers and men and women of god, but they were rascals and thieves and miscreants too for they were Brummies and this is no fairy story but a story of human beings.

Earlier that evening a seventeen-year-old boy called Malcolm Smith and his next-door neighbour Mary O'Malley had spent two hours walking around town. Malcolm had worn his hair slicked with the last finger scrapings of a jar of Bryllcream, to The Right Side, just like the fella in the latest Picture Post; Mary, who was a year older, had modelled her favourite lemon-yellow halter-neck dress. They'd had a cup of tea in Rackhams just before the iron shutters of the paternoster came down and then they'd walked around the flagstones of St Philip's. Along the length of New Street they'd talked about the comings and goings of the world and where they might lead – "some days you hear about the

71

Russians coming to help," said Malcolm, "sometimes it's the Yanks"– and about the history of the city in which they lived – "my great grandfather came here a hundred years ago," said Mary, "he laid the first stone of the free library, or so my dad says." Mention of the past made them feel secure at first, but then a sense of uncertainty re-entered the conversation and the pace of their walking increased. They were at the markets by St Martins when the bombs began to fall.

At once, the sky above their heads was lit up and the ground began to tremble beneath their feet. Their conversation jolted. How would they get home in one piece? The two of them lived on Garrison Lane, in Small Heath. The boy said:

"Shall we go under the railway bridge, along the Coventry Road?"

And the girl said: "That won't be safe. Don't forget they bombed the market hall. We should go this way instead."She led them to the library and they set off for the comparative darkness of the backstreets of Deritend. Malcolm and Mary were passing the Fountain pub when it was hit with a high explosive bomb. Inside, eight people died; on the pavement Malcolm and Mary were caught in the blast and blown into smithereens. And that was nearly the end of this story of Birmingham before it had properly begun. But a strange thing happened on that night in 1940...

When the bomb exploded, a cloud of dust was sucked up into the incendiary-lit night. It mushroomed like a cataclysm above the blackened Brummie brick and earth. Malcolm and Mary were in the cloud, of course. They were there in atoms and motes of matter, but there was something else of them in the mushroom too, in Malcolm's last words – "it's scary isn't it?" – and Mary's reply – "it'll be ok, just you see" – something intangible, transcendent, their essence perhaps, or even – and whisper this, for this is no fairy tale – their souls. And that was only the start of it. For above the city, over the days and weeks that followed, a unique event unfolded, a confluence of fate and meteorology the like of which had never been seen.

The fleets of aeroplanes that had crossed sea and land to bring destruction to Birmingham had stirred the sky itself. They'd created wakes and drafts and currents that flowed into streams and rivers of air and these had carried to the city the matter and souls of people from places faraway. One such trail came from a town in India, in the province of Kashmir. As the bombers took off, fourteen-year-old Rauf Rashid Raza was stripping the engine from a BSA Sloper; cutting his thumb on a circlip, he began to swear. Another came from Krakow in Poland, where Zofia Dornbaum was being given her first taste of solid food. She choked on a cake of buckwheat groats and when her young mother panicked and bashed her heavily on her back, Zofia cried out in alarm. Yet another came from Jamaica and from Worthy Park Estate. There, Charles Maclaren sat in his office on the day before his last as an employee of the sugar factory. It was hot that afternoon, on the edge of the jungle, sweatily, tropically hot, and the humidity was high. Sitting at his desk, the old accountant reached out and touched the photograph of his wife that watched him work; closing his eyes he shook his head and sang a song from their childhood together:

"Mongoose go down Missa Beckford kitchen,

Tek out one a 'im ritious chicken,

Put im inna 'im wasicoat pocket.

Run mongoose."

And so a drop of blood and a truncated oath from Mirpur, a speck of saliva and a bawl from Podgordze, a flick of sweat and a song from the parish of St Anne were borne to Birmingham by a freakish fate. And there they commingled in the great cloud that formed above the ruins of Deritend.

Days passed. Weeks, months. The cloud lingered in the air, in molecules, the cloud diffused. It was blown by gusts and breezes. It fell to ground, as dew. It rained into the River Rea. It soaked into the earth, into parks and gardens all across the city. In the years that followed the war, Birmingham was rebuilt. Out of bomb pecks grew roads and shops and houses, and their concrete and tarmac and mortar contained the matter and souls of Mary O'Malley and Malcolm Smith, of Rauf Rashid Raza, Zofia Dornbaum and Charles Maclaren. And then, in time, the cousins of Mary, the neighbours of Rauf, the sons and daughters of Zofia and the grandchildren of Charles came to live in this new Birmingham. They were industrious and generous and kind-hearted people, but they were feckless and criminal and dishonest too, for this is no fairy tale but a story of human beings (it had been said, by-the-by, that Mary was wilful and Malcolm was sly, that Rauf was a burden, Zofia a trial; and Charles, well, Charles was a loner, prone to extremes of mood, not quite right in the head.) And they found in Birmingham a city not just of a secure and diverting past but a city of a human and uncertain future, a city that was ugly, glorious, troubled, beautiful, a city that was of this earth and of this world, a city that was home...

# TAKING TAPAS ON THE TERRACE

George stands on his rooftop terrace and looks down over the city. It is nearly time for his guests to arrive and he is feeling bullish. Every movement on the streets below affirms the measure he has of this world and his place in it and as he plays out the evening's scenarios in his head, he smiles. He has been looking forward to tonight for some time.

The intercom sounds and he goes back inside. After buzzing his friends in, he fixes himself a gin and tonic and a bowl of habas fritas and waits in the doorway of the apartment.

"Tim! Maddy! Lovely to see you! You got in OK then?"

"We managed to get past those heavily armed teenagers downstairs, if that's what you mean," says Tim.

"Ah, Abdi and Guleed! They create an impression, don't they? They're going to be here until the gate's fixed. They fought in the war."

"Which one?" says Maddy.

"Do you know I completely forgot to ask? Africa somewhere, I imagine."

"Started early I see."

"Au contraire! You bring out the best in me, that's all." George grins, winks. "Did you find us alright?"

"Yes," says Tim, "though we had to take a detour on the other side of the park."

"I thought I heard something! Bloody fireworks!"

"Not exactly. Haven't you seen? There's been more trouble. In fact it's still going on. Here, do you want to see?"

Tim takes out his phone. George waves his hand.

"No, I'm good thanks. I imagine it's the same as it was last week, last month, last year. Nothing changes does it? I sometimes wonder what the point of it is."

"You're right," says Maddy, "it's such a frightful bore."

Tim raises his eyebrows in Maddy's direction, Maddy ignores him and George broadens his smile; he is delighted that Maddy has arrived in the mood to do battle. As the three of them move past the marble table and leather sofas of the apartment's reception area, they are met by Emma, George's wife. She greets Maddy with a squeeze of her arm and ushers her away for the tour.

"Seriously though," says Tim, when the women are out of earshot, "you might want to get onto someone about your gate. How long has it been like that?"

"Not sure. A day? Two days?"

"You're not bothered? With all this going on?"

"Not in the slightest. Nothing's going to happen, is it? Besides, Abdi and Guleed aren't here to make up the numbers. I'd like to see anyone try it on with those two, I can tell you."

"OK. But if it's all the same to you, I'm going to keep an eye on things. We're going to need to know the best route home."

"Oh, it'll have fizzled out long before we're done, I can assure you. Speaking of, can I get you gin and tonic? Start as we mean to go on?"

Now it is Tim's turn to smile. George is irresistible when he's in this mood. He is right, too. There's no need to read too much into the disturbances at the best of times and certainly not on a night like tonight, when there are celebrations to be had. "I don't see why not!" he says, and as he feels his phone vibrate again, he switches it to silent.

\*

Maddy and Emma are on the terrace, sipping gin and tonic. Emma is hymning the view. On the horizon, the far side of the river is lined with tall towers of steel and glass that glint in the evening sun; extending from the near bank are densely packed rooves of houses, stripes of treetops, a patch of dusty green. "You can just about see the lake. Look – over there between the trees. It was one of the reasons we bought here. So many memories."

Maddy knows the lake well. George once rowed her to the island, where they had champagne and slices of home-made tortilla. Despite herself the recollection makes her visibly reflective – disbelief giving way to indignation – and Emma puts a hand on her arm. "I'm glad you came tonight, Mads. I know the boys have been seeing a lot of each other but it's been a while, hasn't it? And we did wonder if you'd fancy it. What with the result and everything."

Maddy registers Emma's condescension with barely a flicker of resentment. Emma has clearly taken her cue from George, but her attempt to unsettle Maddy is obvious and ineffectual. "Oh please, don't worry about that. We arranged this months ago. It just didn't dawn on us it was the day after the election. Nor that he was going to win."

"That's true. But you and George. You do seem to rub each other up the wrong way when it comes to politics."

"Only politics? Honestly, it's OK, really it is. We've known each other a long time. I know he doesn't mean anything by it. He just can't help himself."

"You're right. I just thought…well, you know. This whole election has been…it's been difficult. He's…was a divisive candidate. Some of the things George has told me about him! But it doesn't mean he's wrong. Please try to remember that."

Maddy frowns. For all that Emma is a minor irritant, the charade is becoming painful. "I don't really want to talk about it."

"OK, but promise me you'll speak to Tim about the ins-and-outs when you get the chance. I know we've had our differences, but I'd hate us to fall out over this. George still thinks the world of you, you know."

"I'd have thought falling out with me would have been the least of his worries," scoffs Maddy.

"What do you mean?"

"Oh, just that there's a lot of Abdi and Guleeds out there tonight, that's all. A lot of unhappy people."

"I know! It's awful isn't it? But try not to take on so. Come on. Let me show you the kitchen."

Emma smiles and, placing a hand on Maddy's back, guides her back inside. As Maddy swallows her ire, there is a dull thud behind them and a wisp of smoke rises above the trees in the park.

*

The four friends sit on the terrace around a glass-topped table, eating tapas. The chef has excelled himself: there are chicken livers and prawns and padron peppers, there are slices of ham and sausage, mussels and a salad with cod; the plentiful wine has been carefully chosen and chilled to just the right degree. The conversation too, is taking the form that George had hoped it would: with Emma and Tim providing an obliging audience, he has goaded Maddy by repeatedly raising the subject of the election. True, Maddy has so far denied him the pleasure of rising to his provocation but it is only a matter of time. With the appearance of a bottle of patxaran, George decides to be more direct. "To the mayor!" he says, and winks at Tim. Now the battle is joined.

Maddy shakes her head. "I'm glad you're finding all this so funny."

"You never used to mind."

"Mind what?"

"Oh you know. Us ribbing each other, having a bit of a giggle."

"That was a lifetime ago, George. Times change. There's plenty of people struggling to make light of your mayor just now. Those are police helicopters over there, or haven't you noticed?"

"Really? And what of it?"

"That's right — you go right ahead and underestimate us. Just like you always do."

"Us? And who's us? That would be you and the rioters would it?"

"Well I've got more in common with them than I have with you."

"Nonsense!" George sweeps his arm in a gesture that is both extravagant and derisive. "Look around you. Go on. You do know you can't actually pick and choose your side don't you? I mean you do understand that?"

"You'd like to think that, wouldn't you? That this is the natural order of things."

"Why fight it? We are the winners, after all. We're always going to be the winners."

"You're wrong."

An idea comes to George. "OK. Let me put it another way. You see these mussels – do you like them?"

"What on earth has that got to do with anything?"

"They're from Catalonia. The St Ebro River. They're the finest mussels that money can buy."

Maddy can see what is coming. The argument is tired but she has drunk too much wine to respond with the necessary wit. She tries to buy a little time. "What's your point?"

"You first had them about twenty-five years ago. Do you remember? We were drinking ratafia, in that bar in Barca. And here you are, having them again. So don't tell me I'm wrong and times change because they don't. And neither do we. Unless…" He pauses, cocking his head in theatrical consternation. "Unless you've stopped liking the mussels. You haven't stopped liking the mussels have you? Because you seem to be enjoying them well enough."

"This is ridiculous. Utterly ridiculous."

"Just answer the question," grins George, looming. "Are you enjoying the mussels? That's all I'd like to know."

Tim sniggers and Emma suppresses a smile. Maddy has been outmanoeuvred, by the wine, by the occasion. Worse, the space where logic should be is filled with a meaningless guilt, because the mussels are so very good. She pushes her plate away and stands up from the table, with nothing but defiance left.

"Fuck you George. Do you know what? I don't even know what I'm doing here."

"That's enough," says Tim.

"And fuck you too. You're worse than he is. At least George has some balls."

"Maddy!" says Emma as Tim looks to George for support. But George has been distracted and doesn't give it.

"Quiet a minute," he says, putting a finger to his lips, looking over his shoulder. "Did anyone hear that?"

He crosses to the edge of the terrace. Everyone stops to listen. They hear traffic and in the distance there are sirens, but there is something else, something more distinct and urgent. It is a commotion from the streets below, breaking glass and voices, shrieks and angry people shouting. "That sounds very close," says Tim and he checks his phone. "My god! They're through the park."

There is confusion around the table. "George?" says Emma as Tim pales and Maddy lurches from alarm to delight and back again. Only George remains calm. Holding his hands up to reassure his guests, he crosses to the intercom and switches on a small screen. "There's nothing to worry about, really there isn't. Abdi and Guleed will take care of this."

The screen flickers into life. It shows the gates to the complex, broken and open, then an empty security hut. There is no sign of the two Africans and no one answers the intercom. "They're not going to come here are they?" says Emma. "I mean they won't get that far will they?"

From the street below comes gunfire; first a single shot, then more, one after the other, in a concentrated burst.

"No," says George. "Of course not. I mean they can't. There must be some mistake."

But for the first time tonight, he sounds unsure.

# Author Biography

Charlie Hill is the critically-acclaimed author of three novels – *The Space Between Things*, *Books* and *The Pirate Queen* – and a memoir – *I Don't Want to go to the Taj Mahal*. This is his first collection of short stories.

Charlie lives in Birmingham. He is a Fellow of the Royal Literary Fund.

# Acknowledgements and Thanks

With thanks to Isabelle at Fly on the Wall Press, and to (endorsers in here). And, as ever, to Andrea.

The following stories in the collection have previously appeared in magazines and journals in print and online.

Work – Ambit, 2017

When Helen Levitt met Vivian Maier – Fictive Dream, 2022

Pulling Together – Ink, Sweat & Tears, 2022

A modern history of the Levant – East of the Web, 2017

The state of us – Litro, 2014 (reprinted by the Ikon Gallery, 2016)

Taking tapas on the terrace – Litro, 2020

## About Fly on the Wall Press

A publisher with a conscience.
*Political, Sustainable, Ethical.*
Publishing politically-engaged, international fiction, poetry and cross-genre anthologies on pressing issues. Founded in 2018 by founding editor, Isabelle Kenyon.

## Some other publications:

*The Sound of the Earth Singing to Herself by Ricky Ray*

*We Saw It All Happen by Julian Bishop*

*Odd as F\*ck by Anne Walsh Donnelly*

*Imperfect Beginnings by Viv Fogel*

*These Mothers of Gods by Rachel Bower*

*Sin Is Due To Open In A Room Above Kitty's by Morag Anderson*

*Fauna by David Hartley*

*How To Bring Him Back by Clare HM*

*Hassan's Zoo and A Village in Winter by Ruth Brandt*

*No One Has Any Intention of Building A Wall by Ruth Brandt*

*Snapshots of the Apocalypse by Katy Wimhurst*

*Demos Rising*

*Exposition Ladies by Helen Bowie*

*A Dedication to Drowning by Maeve McKenna*

*The House with Two Letterboxes by Janet H Swinney*

*Climacteric by Jo Bratten*

*Cracked Asphalt by Sree Sen*

Social Media:

@fly_press (Twitter) @flyonthewallpress (Instagram)

@flyonthewallpress (Facebook)

www.flyonthewallpress.co.uk